# The Candy Egg Bunny

LIBRARY OF CONGRESS CATALOGING IN PUBLICATION DATA

Weil, Lisl.
  The candy egg bunny.

  SUMMARY: A little boy discovers the reason bunnies
bring eggs at Easter time.
  [1.  Easter stories]    I.  Title.
PZ7.W433Can  [E]                74-19041
  ISBN 0-8234-0250-9

Weekly Reader Children's Book Club presents

# The Candy Egg Bunny

written and illustrated by

## Lisl Weil

### Holiday House
### New York

Weekly Reader Children's Book Club Edition

"Spring is here," said Sally, "and it's time again
for the Candy Egg Bunny to bring us some eggs."

"There's no such thing as a Candy Egg Bunny,"
said Walter. "Candy Egg Bunnies are make-believe."
"That's what *you* think," said Sally.

When Walter looked up, he saw a big bunny
standing next to him.

"Come on, you're not for real," Walter laughed.
"We are real, as long as children
want us to be," answered the big bunny, smiling.
"But bunnies don't make eggs, birds do.
Everyone knows that," said Walter.

"Listen," said the bunny with a kind voice.
"A long time ago, on top of a hill . . .

there lived the evil witch Gundula.

At night, Gundula would fly about scaring people
and doing her·evil tricks and spells.
Her favorite trick was to change people into animals.

Of course, evil witches work only at night.
That's why Gundula loved to sleep during the day.

She also loved a sweet snack of jelly beans and candy
before going to bed.

But one day,
Gundula could not fall asleep.

Right in front of her window was a tree.
In the tree was a nest. In the nest were eggs.

And now baby birds had hatched from the eggs.
Their peeping and chirping kept Gundula awake.

For days, Gundula tried to get rid of the noise,
but nothing seemed to help. The happy birds
just chirped and peeped louder than ever.

She was just too tired at night to fly about
doing her evil tricks and spells.

But tired as she was, Gundula decided
to get rid of the birds now and forever.

That night, to be extra safe, Gundula used
her double-evil spell.

"Beaks to whiskers
and feathers to fur,
hops to leaps,
no more peeps!"
she chanted twice.

Gundula was pleased with her handiwork.
The birds had turned into bunnies.

And bunnies don't peep or chirp.
At last, Gundula could sleep all day.

How mistaken she was, because bunnies hop!

And hop they did, all over the evil witch.

The bunnies followed Gundula

wherever she

tried to hide.

This time Gundula had had enough.
She flew away, leaving behind the jelly beans
and candy in her cellar.

And no one has heard of her since.

The people were happy to be free of the evil witch and came to thank the bunnies. And the bunnies were happy being bunnies.

It was the beginning of a new life for everyone.

So the bunnies decided to have a party—just like a birthday party.

"But what is a party without gifts?" they asked.
Then they thought of the candy in Gundula's cellar.
And they remembered what they used to be
before they were birds—eggs! Why not stuff some eggs
full of jelly beans for the party?

The big bunny smiled at Walter as he ended his story.
"My great-great-grandfather was one of those special
bunnies," he said. "Since then, we Candy Egg Bunnies are
very busy at this time of year. Excuse me, now, I'm
really late . . ."

When Walter looked up again, the big bunny
had disappeared.

"I must have been dreaming," said Walter loudly
to himself.

"That's what *you* think," said Sally.